HI I'M ROWLEY JEFFERSON.

HERE ARE SOME BOOKS MY BEST FRIEND GREG HEFFLEY WROTE.

THE DIARY OF A WIMPY KID SERIES

YEAH AND THEN YOU TOTALLY STOLE MY IDEA!

DIARY OF AN

I WROTE THE WORDS AND DREW THE PICTURES ALL BY MYSELF WITHOUT ANY HELP FROM A GROWN-UP!

Rowley Jefferson's JOURNAL

by Jeff Kinney

THORNDIKE PRESS

A part of Gale, a Cengage Company

GALE
A Cengage Company

Farmington Hills, Mich • Andover, UK • Chicago • Mason, Ohio
Meriden, Conn • New York • San Francisco • Singapore • Waterville, Maine

OK THEN WHO'S THIS GUY?

Recommended for Middle Readers.

Awesome Friendly Kid text and illustrations copyright © 2018, 2019, Wimpy Kid, Inc. DIARY OF AN AWESOME FRIENDLY KID™, ROWLEY JEFFERSON'S JOURNAL™, the Greg Heffley design™, and the design of the book's jacket are trademarks and trade dress of Wimpy Kid, Inc. All rights reserved.

Thorndike Press, a part of Gale, a Cengage Company

Thorndike Press® Large Print Middle Reader.

The text of this Large Print edition is unabridged.

Other aspects of the book may vary from the original edition.

Set in 16 pt. Plantin.

LIBRARY OF CONGRESS CIP DATA ON FILE
CATALOGUING IN PUBLICATION FOR THIS BOOK
IS AVAILABLE FROM THE LIBRARY OF CONGRESS

ISBN-13: 978-1-4328-6634-1 (hardcover alk. paper)

Published in 2019 by arrangement with Amulet Books, an imprint of Harry N. Abrams, Inc.

Printed in Mexico
1 2 3 4 5 6 7 23 22 21 20 19

<u>My First Entry</u>

Hi I'm Rowley Jefferson and this is my diary. I hope you like it so far.

I decided to start a journal because my best friend Greg Heffley has one and we usually do the same stuff. Oh yeah I should mention that me and Greg are

I'm sure you're probably like "Well tell me more about this Greg guy." But my book isn't about HIM, it's about ME.

The reason I called my book Diary of an Awesome Friendly Kid is because that's what my dad is always saying about me.

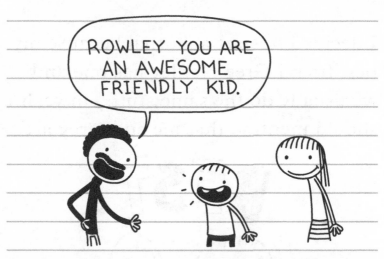

Like I mentioned already, Greg is my best friend which makes my dad my SECOND best friend. But I don't tell him that because I don't want to hurt his feelings.

Now that I brought up my dad I should mention he doesn't seem to like Greg all that much. And the reason I get that feeling is because my dad is always saying it.

But that's only because my dad doesn't really get Greg's sense of humor.

Right now you're probably thinking "Hey Rowley I thought this book was supposed to be about YOU." Well you're right so from now on I promise there's gonna be a lot more Rowley in here.

The first thing you need to know about me is that I live with my mom and dad in a house at the top of Surrey Street, which is the same street my best friend Greg lives on.

I already talked about my dad but my mom is pretty great too because she feeds me healthy food and helps me keep my body clean.

SCRUB
SCRUB

Every morning I walk to school with my friend Greg. We usually have a total blast when we're together but sometimes I do things that annoy him.

But what REALLY gets on Greg's nerves is when I copy him. So I'm probably not gonna let him know about this journal because it's just gonna make him mad.

Anyway writing in this book is a lot of work so that's all I'm gonna do for today. But tomorrow I'll put a little more Greg in here because like I said we're best friends.

My Second Entry

OK so bad news: Greg found out about my diary.

I guess I felt kind of proud that I had my own journal and I wanted to show him. But just like I predicted it made him MAD.

Greg said I totally ripped him off and that he was gonna sue me for stealing his idea. I said well go ahead and TRY because you're not the FIRST person to write in a diary.

Then Greg said it's a JOURNAL not a
diary and then he whapped me with my
own book.

I told Greg if he was gonna be a jerk then
I wouldn't say nice things about him in
my journal. Then I showed him what I
wrote so far.

At first he seemed annoyed because I
always forget to draw noses on people.
But then he said my book gave him an
IDEA.

Greg said one day he's gonna be rich and
famous and everyone will want to know
his whole life's story. And he said I could
be the one to WRITE it.

I said I thought that's what your JOURNAL is for and he said that's his AUTObiography but my book could be his BIOGRAPHY.

Greg said there are gonna be a LOT of biographies about him one day but he'd give me the chance to write the first one.

I thought that sounded like a good idea because I'm Greg's best friend and no one knows him better than ME.

So I'm gonna start this book over with a new title and now the main character is gonna be Greg instead of me. But don't worry I'm still gonna be in it a lot too.

DIARY OF **GREG HEFFLEY**

by Greg Heffley's Best Friend

Rowley Jefferson →

EARLY LIFE

Most biographies about presidents and famous people start with a chapter called "Early Life." Well the problem is that I didn't meet Greg until the fourth grade so I don't know a lot about what happened to him before then.

I've seen a few photos hanging on the walls in Greg's house and from what I can tell he was a regular baby. And if he did anything important when he was little you can't really tell from the pictures.

Anyway fast-forward to right before the start of fourth grade and now this biography is gonna get a lot more detailed.

We used to live in a whole different state but then my dad got a job and we had to move. My family bought a new house at the top of Surrey Street and we moved in over the summer.

The first few days I didn't leave the house because I was scared about being in a new place.

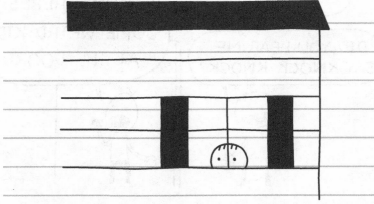

I know you are probably wondering "Well when is he going to meet Greg?" but just wait because I am getting to that part.

My mom said maybe I should try to make some friends and she even bought me a book called "How to Make Friends in New Places" to help me do it.

The book had all kinds of things like knock-knock jokes to help a kid like me meet new people. But the tricks in the book didn't really work on Greg.

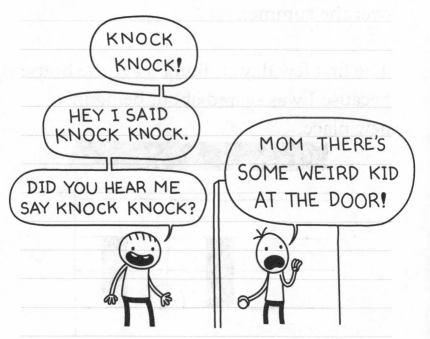

Luckily me and Greg became friends anyway.

I told Greg I lived in the new house at the top of the hill and he said that was kind of bad news for me because when our lot was empty he planted a flag there so now he owned my house plus everything in it.

But later on my dad told me that wasn't true and then he went to Greg's house to get my bike back.

I'm pretty sure that's the first time my dad told me what he thought about Greg.

But I like Greg a LOT. He is always doing hilarious things like making me laugh right after I take a big gulp of milk.

Plus Greg is always playing wacky pranks on me and they usually make me laugh pretty hard too.

So I'll bet you can tell why me and Greg have been best friends since fourth grade. I even got us a locket to make it official but Greg says those things are for girls and that's why he won't wear his half.

Well I could probably fill up a whole book with all the zany things me and Greg do but since this is his biography I should probably write some stuff about his family.

Greg has a mom and dad just like I do but they are pretty regular parents so I don't have a lot to say about them.

But Greg isn't an only child like me. He's got an older brother named Rodrick who has a rock band called Loded Diper.

Some of their songs have swears in them so my mom and dad won't let me be at the Heffleys' house when Rodrick has practice.

Greg also has a little brother named Manny who is only three. And don't ask me why but the first time I went to Greg's for a playdate Manny randomly pulled down his pants and showed me his heinie.

Now every time I see Manny he acts like we have this big secret or something which makes me feel uncomfortable.

Anyway I guess that wraps up the first chapter of Greg's biography. And if you're thinking "Rowley when are we gonna get to the exciting parts?" then just WAIT.

THE TIME I HAD MY FIRST SLEEPOVER AT GREG'S

After me and Greg met we had a few playdates at MY house and a few playdates at HIS house. Oh yeah I forgot, Greg doesn't like it when I call them "playdates" so I will have to change that in the next draft or else I'm gonna get whapped again.

Anyway me and Greg "hung out" a lot at each other's houses but then one day he invited me to his house for a SLEEPOVER.

I was pretty worried because I'd never slept away from home before. In fact I wasn't even sleeping in my OWN bed yet because I was scared.

I told my mom I was too nervous to stay at Greg's but I got a little LESS nervous when she said I could take Carrots with me.

When I got to Greg's we played in his room for a while but at 9:00 Mrs. Heffley said it was time to go to bed. And she said we had to sleep in the BASEMENT. Well now I was SUPER nervous because I think basements are really creepy.

As soon as Mrs. Heffley turned the lights off, Greg said he needed to tell me something important. He told me there's a half man, half goat that lives in the woods in our neighborhood so I probably shouldn't go outside alone at night.

Well I was NOT happy to hear that news and I really wished someone told my parents about this goat guy before we moved into the neighborhood.

Anyway the goat thing got me TOTALLY spooked so I hid under the covers. But I think Greg got pretty spooked too because he crawled under them WITH me.

Then all of a sudden there was this crazy noise right outside the window and it sounded exactly how a half man, half goat would sound.

Me and Greg didn't wanna get eaten by this goat guy so we got out of there as fast as we could.

But we almost died anyway because we trampled each other running up the stairs.

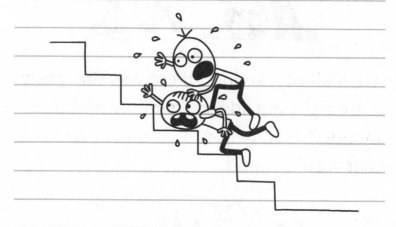

We locked ourselves in the laundry room so the goat man couldn't get us. But that's when we found out it wasn't the goat guy at ALL, it was just Greg's brother Rodrick playing a trick on us.

RAP
RAP

OK this next part is embarrassing but since it's a biography I've gotta tell the whole truth. I wet my pants when we were in the basement and heard those noises outside.

Mrs. Heffley gave me an extra pair of Greg's underwear but they were too small. So my dad had to come get me and bring me home in the middle of the night.

It was a long time before I was allowed to go to Greg's for another sleepover, but that's a MUCH longer story and I'm not even sure there's room for that one in this book.

THE TIME I SAVED GREG FROM TEVIN LARKIN'S BIRTHDAY PARTY

There is a kid named Tevin Larkin who lives over on Speen Street and last summer his mom invited me and Greg to Tevin's birthday party. We didn't wanna go because Tevin is hyper but both of our moms said we HAD to.

It turned out that me and Greg were the ONLY kids invited to Tevin's party but we didn't know that until we got there.

After we gave Tevin his presents his mom said it was time for party activities.

The first activity was to watch this movie about a guy who could turn into a bear and an eagle and a bunch of other animals.

When the movie was over Tevin wanted to watch it AGAIN. But me and Greg told Tevin's mom we didn't wanna watch the movie a second time so she said we could move on to the other activities like pin the tail on the donkey.

Well that just made Tevin MAD.

He got all wound up and started acting like the guy in the movie who could turn into animals.

I guess Tevin's mom was used to this sort of thing but me and Greg didn't know what we were supposed to do. We asked Mrs. Larkin if she could take us home but she said there were still two hours to go in the party.

So we went out the back door and waited in the yard for Tevin to calm down.

But eventually Tevin found us and now he was acting TOTALLY nuts.

I took a few steps back to get out of Tevin's way but that's when I fell into a giant ditch. Luckily the ditch wasn't TOO deep or I probably would've broke some bones. But when I got to my feet I heard this buzzing noise all around me.

It turned out there was a HORNET'S NEST at the bottom of the ditch and they were all stirred up.

I got stung twelve times and two of the stings were inside my MOUTH.

Mrs. Larkin drove me home early and Greg hitched a ride too.

Anyway Greg is always saying he "owes me" for getting him out of that party and I put it in this book in case I ever need to remind him.

GREG'S ACCOMPLISHMENTS

Every biography I've ever read for school has a chapter called "Accomplishments" so I figure I better add that in here before I forget.

The problem is that Greg is only a kid and most of his accomplishments haven't happened yet. So I'll leave some blank space here and I can fill it in later on.

1.
2.
3.
4.
5.
6.
7.
8.
9.
10.

THE TIME ME AND GREG DISTURBED AN ANCIENT BURIAL GROUND

If you were spooked out by that goat man story from before then you might want to skip this one. OK if you are still reading, remember I warned you.

One time me and Greg were playing vikings and ninjas in the woods and then some teenagers came by and ruined our fun.

BUT THAT'S NOT EVEN THE SCARY PART YET so keep reading.

Me and Greg went farther back in the woods to get away from those teens. Greg said we should build a fort so if they came looking for us we could protect ourselves.

So we spent the rest of the afternoon making a fort out of sticks and logs.

Greg said we should put some rocks in our fort in case things got REALLY bad, but it was starting to get dark and there weren't a lot of rocks lying around in the woods anyway.

But then I tripped over something and guess what? It was a big ROCK.

I told Greg I thought I sprained my ankle but he was a lot more worried about that rock than my injury.

Greg said it wasn't a rock, it was a GRAVESTONE and we just disturbed an ANCIENT BURIAL GROUND.

I guess you already knew that was coming because it was in the title of this chapter. I'll probably change it later on so I don't give the surprise away.

Anyway me and Greg were TOTALLY spooked out by this ancient burial ground thing and by now it was REALLY dark out so we were extra scared. But Greg must've totally forgot about my ankle because he took off and I couldn't keep up.

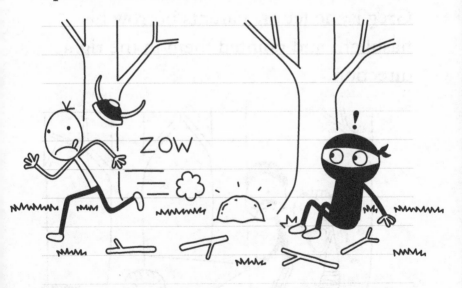

I kept waiting for Greg to come back but he never did.

Luckily my parents called Greg's house to ask where I was and that helped him remember I was still out there.

And just to show you what a great pal Greg is, he let my parents borrow his flashlight and pointed them in the right direction.

DRAG

AN EVEN MORE SCARY STORY

OK while I'm on the topic of scary stuff I want to share a story about something that happened a couple years ago.

One time I was at my grandpa's log cabin with my dad for the weekend and we took a hike and I got kind of dirty. Well technically it's my DAD'S cabin now because my grandpa died the year before.

I called my grandpa "Bampy," and the reason I called him that is because when I was two I couldn't say "Grampa."

BAMPY!

But when I got older and I COULD say "Grampa," nobody would let me change it. And when my grandpa got older it's the only word he really said.

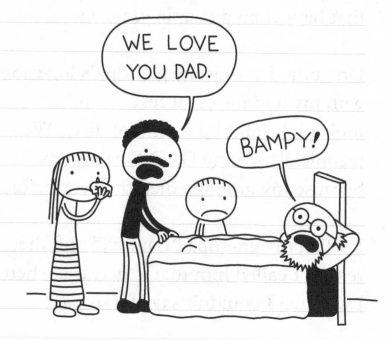

So anyway back to the story. After I got dirty from that hike my dad said I had to take a shower.

But Bampy's cabin is really old and it doesn't HAVE a shower, it just has one of those creepy old-fashioned tubs.

After I filled up the tub with water and got in, here's what happened NEXT. I heard footsteps coming down the hall and I thought it was my dad bringing me a towel or something.

Then the door opened real slow, but guess what? NO ONE WAS EVEN THERE.

I jumped out of the tub and ran around the house looking everywhere for my dad.

And if you're thinking "Oh Rowley the door thing was your dad playing a trick on you," well guess what? It WASN'T.

My dad was getting some milk at the store and he didn't come back until like a half hour later.

I told my dad what happened with the door and he said it was probably just the "wind."

But I know what it was: the GHOST OF BAMPY.

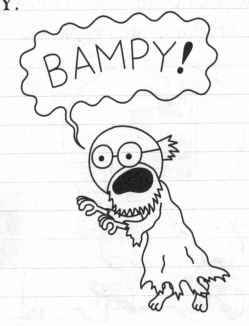

BAMPY!

THE TIME GREG PLAYED A HILARIOUS PRANK ON ME

OK I know the last chapter didn't have a lot of Greg in it but I wanted to mention that story real quick because the Bampy thing totally FREAKED ME OUT.

If you like scary stuff then you're in luck because this one is pretty scary too.

One day me and Greg were hanging out at my house and Greg told me he saw on the news that there was a burglar going around breaking into people's homes.

Then he said he had to go home for dinner, and once he left I started getting scared because my parents weren't around.

But here's the thing: I found out later that Greg just PRETENDED to leave. He shut the front door but then stayed inside my house.

He took off his shoes and walked up the stairs super quiet so I couldn't hear him.

Then he started stomping around real loud upstairs. At first I thought it was the ghost of Bampy all over again.

Then I realized it was probably that BURGLAR Greg told me about and I almost peed my pants for the second time in this biography.

I heard footsteps coming down the stairs and I ran into the garage to hide from the burglar.

It was PITCH BLACK in the garage but I didn't want to make a move until I was sure that guy was gone.

Then all of a sudden the door to the garage opened real slow and I knew the burglar was gonna get me if I didn't do something. So I whacked him in the face with my dad's tennis racket and made a run for it.

WHACK—

Then I ran out the front door and went to Mrs. Monroe's house next door to tell her to call the COPS.

But then Greg came out of my house and that's when I found out the whole thing was just one of his hilarious pranks.

Greg was mad at me for two whole weeks and he said I should've known from the way the footsteps sounded that it was HIM and not a burglar.

I guess he's got a pretty good point about that since he is always playing wacky pranks on me. So I feel kind of bad about whacking him with a tennis racket.

but not really

ANOTHER TIME GREG
GOT MAD AT ME

OK that last story made me remember another time Greg got mad at me.

Me and Greg were walking home from school a few months ago and there were slugs everywhere because it just rained the night before. And whenever there are slugs lying around, Greg chases me with one.

I guess it's pretty funny if you think about it but it's never that funny when it's happening.

Luckily I am really fast when someone is chasing me with a slug so I got away from Greg by climbing up on the big rock in Mr. Yee's front yard.

Greg tried to get me to climb down but I stayed right where I was.

Greg tried to fling the slug at me but he lost his balance and almost fell in a giant puddle in front of the rock. He was stuck and I felt bad for him because he is my best friend after all.

I got down from the rock and tried to help Greg. He told me to pull him back up on his feet but I guess I heard him wrong.

I grabbed him BY his feet and that turned out to be a pretty dumb move.

I didn't know WHAT Greg was gonna do once he got out of that puddle but I didn't wanna stick around to find out. So I ran to my house and locked myself in my room and didn't come out until Greg got called home for dinner.

The next day Greg said he was gonna get me back when I "least expect it." I just hope Greg forgets because when it comes to paybacks he's got a good imagination.

THE TIME WHEN GREG CREATED A SPECIAL AWARD JUST FOR ME

OK the last two chapters were about times Greg got mad at me but this chapter is the total OPPOSITE.

This one's about the time when I did something Greg thought was really awesome so then he did something really awesome for ME.

Anyway this one Saturday last fall me and Greg were supposed to hang out at my house but he said he couldn't because he had to clean his garage. Then he said if I came and helped him we'd be done TWICE as quick. But I said no thanks I'll wait.

Then Greg said if I helped him he'd give me HALF of his Halloween candy.

Well that was a really big deal to me because my parents went through all my candy on Halloween night and they barely let me keep ANYTHING.

But I knew Greg still had a TON of candy because his parents don't make him throw out ANYTHING. So I told him OK I'll be right over.

Cleaning Greg's garage was hard work and it took like three hours.

56

After we were done Greg said OK now
let's go hang out at your place.

I said hey what about that CANDY
and Greg said oh yeah I forgot. But I
knew that was gonna happen because
whenever Greg owes me stuff he forgets.

We went up to Greg's room and he got
his bag of candy out of the closet.

But when he emptied out the bag it was almost all WRAPPERS.

The only things LEFT were three jawbreakers and a little box of raisins. I told Greg he promised me a TON of candy and he said he only promised HALF. Then he said a deal's a deal and he gave me a jawbreaker and the box of raisins.

I told Greg I was gonna tell his MOM.
And then Greg got real worried because
he said his mom would be mad at him
if she found out he ate all his Halloween
candy already.

Greg said he was gonna give me
something WAY better than candy, and
he got out a piece of paper and a pencil
and started drawing at his desk.

When Greg was done he handed me the
piece of paper and here's what was on it.

Greg said Good Boy awards are SUPER
rare and you have to do something really
AWESOME to get one.

He said I was EXTRA lucky because this
was the first ever Good Boy award he'd
ever given out and it was gonna be worth
a lot of money.

Well I knew Greg was just trying to get out of giving me the candy he owed me so I tried to act like I thought this Good Boy award thing was dumb. But somehow Greg could tell I thought it was kind of COOL.

Well that was only the FIRST Good Boy award but I got a lot MORE. For the next few weeks Greg made me one every time I did something awesome for him.

After a while I had a TON of Good Boy awards. And I kept them in a binder in clear plastic sheets so they wouldn't get messed up.

But then I started to feel like maybe my Good Boy awards weren't that rare anymore since I had so MANY of them. Plus Greg was making the new ones a lot quicker than he made that first one and they didn't seem all that special.

So one time when Greg called and asked me to come down and help him rake his yard I told him I couldn't because I had homework.

And Greg said that's too bad because he came up with a totally new kind of Good Boy award and he was sad I wasn't gonna get to see it.

I was like well at least TELL me about it, and Greg said he COULDN'T because it was top secret and he didn't wanna ruin the surprise.

Then he said he was gonna call Scotty Douglas and see if HE wanted to help rake the yard and I said OK I'll be right over.

Well I wish I knew we had to rake the front yard AND the back because it was a lot of work. Plus I had to do it MYSELF because Greg was busy making that new award.

When I was finally done Greg gave me my award and I've gotta say it was even more awesome than I THOUGHT it would be.

This new one was called a SUPER Good Boy award. Greg said one Super Good Boy award was worth FIFTY regular Good Boy awards and I could totally see WHY.

In the next few weeks I earned a BUNCH of Super Good Boy awards but after a while even THOSE didn't seem all that special.

Besides I was spending a lot of time doing stuff for Greg and I wasn't getting my OWN chores done.

But every time I told Greg I didn't need any more Good Boy awards he'd come up with something NEW and then I'd have to have THAT.

After a while I had so many awards that my binder was STUFFED and I couldn't fit new ones in. So I told Greg I wasn't gonna try to earn any more no matter WHAT.

But Greg said that's OK because he made up a whole NEW system and I should probably just recycle my old awards.

I was pretty mad because I worked HARD for those awards and now Greg said they were totally WORTHLESS.

But I was still curious about this new system so I asked him about it. Greg said the new idea was called "Li'l Goodies" and it was a POINT system and there wasn't any paper involved.

Greg said that every time I did something NICE for him I'd get a Li'l Goodie point. And once I got fifty Li'l Goodies I'd get a Fantastic Prize.

I was like OK what's the prize? And Greg said he couldn't tell me but it was under a sheet in his bedroom.

Well I couldn't figure out what was under that sheet but I could GUESS. And a LOT of my guesses were things I really wanted.

So I spent about a month doing lots
of things for Greg and he gave me a
Li'l Goodie point each time, like he
promised.

Eventually I got to fifty Li'l Goodies.
And I told Greg I was ready to turn them
in for that Fantastic Prize.

But Greg told me that since it was the
first day of the month my Li'l Goodie
total got reset back to ZERO. And I said
well you never told me about that rule
and he said well you never ASKED.

I was really MAD and I yanked the sheet
off the Fantastic Prize so I could see
what it was.

But guess what? It was a LAUNDRY BASKET filled with dirty clothes.

I told Greg he was a crummy friend for making me do all that work for a phony prize. But he said the laundry thing was just a TEST to see if I'd peek and that I failed the test.

Then he said the REAL prize was locked in the basement and that now I was gonna have to earn a HUNDRED Li'l Goodies to get it.

All I can say is I'm not a FOOL. I'm gonna take my TIME earning those Li'l Goodies, so if Greg thinks I'm in a rush to get that Fantastic Prize he's gonna be disappointed.

THE TIME I FOUND OUT GREG IS A LOUSY STUDY PARTNER

OK I know this is Greg's official biography and I don't want to put any negative stuff about him in here. But Greg if you are reading this I just need to say you are a TERRIBLE study partner. I hope that doesn't hurt your feelings but somebody has to tell you the truth.

Most of the time I don't really need to study for tests because I pay attention in class and I do my homework. Plus Mom always says it's important to get a good night's sleep so on school nights I go to bed extra early.

But this one time we had a really hard chapter in math and I had trouble paying attention in class that week. That's mostly because Greg moved to the seat right behind me.

The night before the test I knew I was gonna have to go over the chapter and do some practice problems at home. But when I told Greg my plan he said we should study TOGETHER.

I wasn't sure that was such a good idea because when it comes to school stuff sometimes it's hard for Greg to focus.

But Greg said we're best friends and best friends should study together so I guess that made sense to me.

Well the FIRST thing we had to do was find a place to study. Greg said we couldn't be at HIS house because his brother Rodrick was having band practice.

And Greg was banned from MY house because he played a practical joke where he put plastic wrap over our toilet bowl and he got my dad pretty good.

GAAAAH!

HEE HEE HEE!

Greg said we should go to the LIBRARY
because it was quiet there and nobody
would bug us. So Mrs. Heffley gave us
a ride to the library after dinner and we
found a table where we could do our work.

We got out our books and I said maybe
we should do practice problems to see
what we needed to work on. But Greg
said he hadn't even READ the chapter
yet so we needed to start from the
BEGINNING.

Well that was kind of a waste of time
for me so I told Greg he could read
the chapter on his OWN to catch up.
But Greg said I was being a bad study
partner and that we were supposed to do
everything TOGETHER.

I said OK fine let's start from the beginning of the chapter and go through the whole thing. But Greg said before we got started we needed to plan our study breaks so we didn't get too stressed out.

Then he said we should START with a break so we'd get off on the right foot. And that's what we did even though it seemed like a bad idea to me.

FLICK

After like ten minutes I said we need to get to work because it's a long chapter and we have a lot to go through.

Well don't ask me why but Greg pinched
his nose with his fingers and said the
same exact thing I said but with a really
annoying voice.

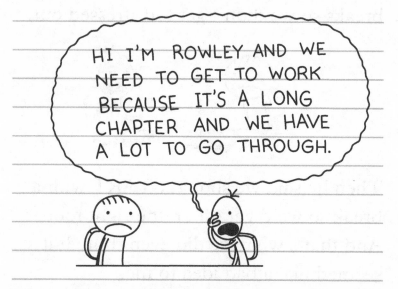

I told Greg to stop copying me but that
just made him copy me even MORE.

Finally I got smart and started reading the chapter out loud.

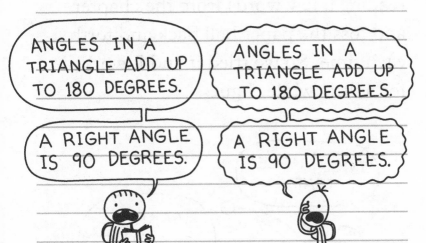

After a while Greg figured out what I was doing and he stopped copying me.

I told him maybe it would be better if we both just read the chapter quietly, but Greg said that wasn't his "learning style" and he needed to make things FUN so they would stick.

I said what do you mean? And Greg said he knew a way to make learning math into a GAME.

First he balled up a piece of notebook paper. He said we should take turns reading a few words from the chapter and toss the paper ball back and forth each time. So we tried it and it worked for a little while, I guess.

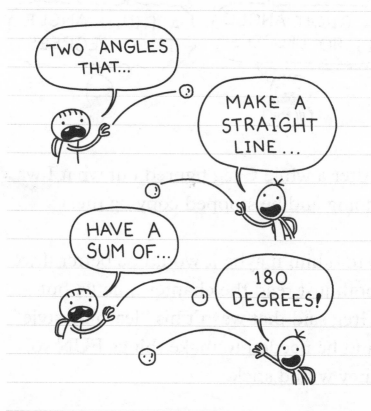

But whenever someone DROPPED the paper ball Greg said we had to start the whole page OVER.

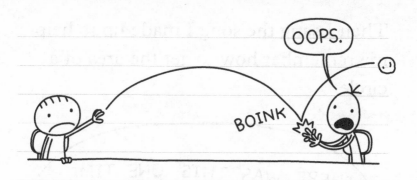

And sometimes I think Greg was trying
to make me drop the ball on PURPOSE.

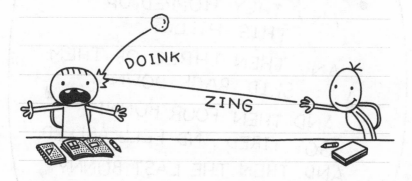

I told Greg we were wasting too much
time and we needed to do this another
way. And Greg said he didn't care HOW
we studied as long as it was FUN.

So I told Greg a trick my dad taught
ME. He said that whenever I had trouble
remembering something I should make
up a SONG to make it easier.

Then I sang the song I made up to help me remember how to get the area of a circle.

Greg said that was the dumbest thing he ever heard and I said well if it's so dumb then why do I have a 95 in math and you only have a 72?

I guess Greg didn't have a good answer to that and he said it was time for another break. So we played video games on the library computer until some grown-up reported us to the librarian for making too much noise.

When we got back to the table Greg said
we weren't studying the right way and
that he had an idea of how we could do it
BETTER. He said he'd read the FIRST
half of the chapter and I'd read the
LAST half and then we could team up
during the test.

I said well you're not allowed to TALK
during the test so I didn't see how that
was gonna work. Then Greg told me
about these monks who can transmit
their thoughts through the air if they
concentrate real hard.

So we tried doing it but I guess I couldn't concentrate good enough to make it work.

Greg said we needed to figure out a DIFFERENT way to communicate during the test.

I said if we just studied the chapter we wouldn't NEED to communicate, but once Greg gets something in his head he doesn't let it go.

He made up this whole system of sneezes and coughs and stuff so we could talk to each other during the test without our teacher Ms. Beck noticing. But there was a lot to remember so I wrote it all down.

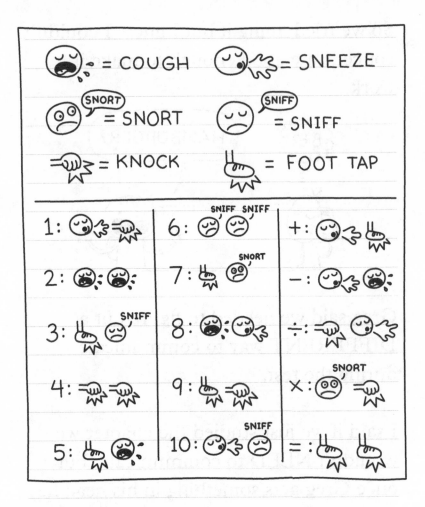

I said well what if one of us needs to ask the other guy a QUESTION and Greg said you just put a question mark at the end. And I said well we don't have a signal for a question mark and Greg said it could be a fart.

I told Greg I didn't think I could fart if I didn't really NEED to and Greg told me to try anyway and I did but nothing came out.

So Greg told me some different foods I could eat for breakfast that would make it easier to do a question mark.

But that idea made me nervous because the last time I went to Greg's we drank a bunch of soda and tried to burp the alphabet, and I got sick on the letter "B" and had to go home early.

Greg said OK if I couldn't fart for REAL then it would be OK to make a fake fart noise under my arm.

That's when I told Greg I thought this was a bad idea and it was CHEATING to send each other signals during the test.

Greg said I was being a goody-two-shoes and that the only reason I wanted to get a good grade in math was because I was a teacher's pet and I was in love with Ms. Beck.

I said I was NOT in love with Ms. Beck but that I just like her personality and the way she smells.

So Greg said that PROVES I'm in love with Ms. Beck and then he sang that song about two people sitting in a tree.

I knew Greg was trying to make me mad but for some reason the song didn't really bother me that much.

I guess Greg got mad that he wasn't making ME mad so he started singing even MORE.

I tried to tune him out but he just got louder and louder.

Then I went into the bathroom and tried to study in THERE but Greg followed me.

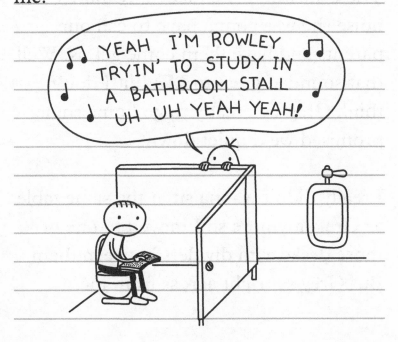

But I guess somebody else complained because the librarian came in and told us we both had to get out of there.

Then she said if we made any more noise she was gonna have to call our parents and have them come get us. Well that sounded great to ME but I don't think Greg was ready to go home so he promised we'd quiet down.

I really didn't wanna sit at the same table as Greg anymore so I moved to one of those desks with dividers between them. But Greg sat right across from me.

I was starting to get some work done but
then Greg slid a note under the divider.

He had a math question so I answered
him and passed the note back.

Hey Rowley
what do the
angles in a
quadrilateral
add up to?

-Greg

360
degrees.

-R

And then Greg asked me ANOTHER
question. But I didn't really mind
because this was a MILLION times
better than the way we were doing things
before.

But then Greg slid the note back and it had another question on it that didn't have anything to do with math at ALL.

Check one. I am embarrassed I wet the bed last night.

☐ YES

☐ NO

Well I checked the NO box because I DIDN'T wet the bed. I slid the note to Greg but then he wrote something on it and slid it BACK.

☐ YES

☒ NO

Ha ha ha you're not embarrassed you wet the bed.

That made me kind of mad because that's not what I MEANT. But I didn't wanna spend a lot of time explaining myself because I really needed to get back to studying.

So Greg wrote ANOTHER note and slid it under the divider.

Truth or Dare?

☐ TRUTH   ☐ DARE

I didn't wanna take a dare from Greg so I picked TRUTH. But I didn't like the question Greg came up with.

☒ TRUTH   ☐ DARE

Are you in love with Ms. Beck?

OK I switch to Dare.

Then Greg dared me to get him a soda from the vending machine. I didn't know that was the way truth or dare WORKED but I was just glad Greg didn't make me answer that question.

After I got Greg his soda I did a little more studying but then he started up with the notes again.

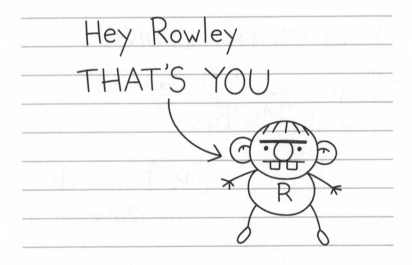

Well I didn't like THAT so I sent back a drawing of my OWN.

And then Greg drew another picture of ME and I drew another one of HIM.

After a while we filled up two whole PAGES with drawings.

Greg tried to start a NEW page of drawings but I just ignored him. And I guess he didn't like that because he kept trying to get my attention.

I decided to move to a new spot that wasn't so close to Greg. I was glad I could finally get some peace and quiet but THAT didn't last long.

If you're wondering what that "bang" was all about, well here's what happened. When I got up and moved to another desk some grown-up took my spot. And I guess Greg thought it was still ME and he tied the guy's shoes together.

Then when the guy stood up he fell backward.

After that happened Greg got out of there as fast as he could. I figured I'd better get out of there TOO because I didn't want that guy to think I was the one who tied his shoes together.

I followed Greg into the children's section where there was an empty table. He put his stuff at one end and I sat down at the other so I didn't have to be too close to him.

Greg said we should take another study break but I said I was gonna keep working. Then Greg balled up a piece of paper and tried to throw it in the trash can across the room.

He missed but he kept shooting balled-up pieces of paper which made it hard for me to concentrate.

Then Greg finally made a basket and he said he bet I couldn't make the same shot as him. But when I told him I really needed to study he said I was too scared to try and then he started acting like a CHICKEN.

I tried to ignore him but it wasn't so easy, ESPECIALLY when he got up on the table.

Then all of a sudden Greg sat down on the table and started making grunting noises. At first I thought he might be having a bathroom emergency. But when he got up there was an EGG.

Well I didn't want Greg to lay another
egg so I balled up a piece of paper and
tossed it at the trash can. And I wasn't
looking to see if it went in but I guess it
DID.

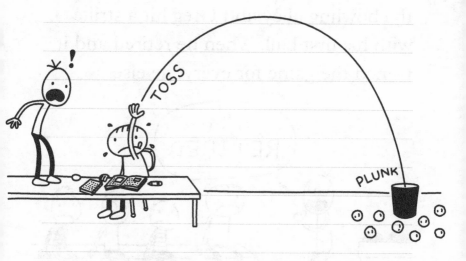

Greg said my shot was total LUCK and
there was no WAY I could make it again
even if I tried a thousand times. But I
decided I wasn't GONNA try again.

Greg said I COULDN'T retire but I said yeah I COULD. And it was his own fault for giving me the idea anyway.

One time I had my birthday party at the bowling alley and Greg hit a strike with his first ball. Then he retired and it ruined the game for everyone else.

When Greg couldn't get me to UN-retire he tried making a backward shot HIMSELF. But he went through like a million pieces of notebook paper and he couldn't even come CLOSE. I was just glad he was leaving me alone because I was getting a lot of work done.

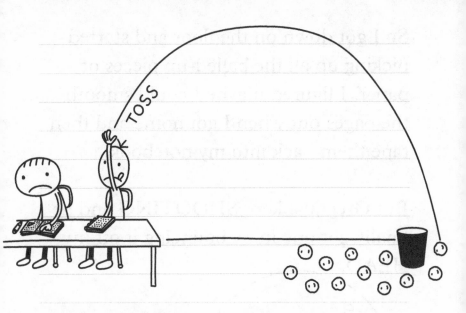

I finished the practice test and then I was
gonna go over my notes from class. But
that's when I found out Greg was getting
all his paper from MY NOTEBOOK.

Well that made me really mad because
Ms. Beck said we were allowed to look at
our notes during the TEST.

So I got down on the floor and started picking up all the balled-up pieces of paper. I figured maybe I could smooth the pages out when I got home and then tape them back into my notebook.

But Greg just kept SHOOTING and he finally got one in by bouncing it off my HEAD.

Well that made me really mad and I started chasing Greg with that egg he laid.

But I guess we were making too much noise and that got us in trouble with the librarian again.

She made me call my parents to come
get us and that was fine with ME.

I had to stay up two more hours
uncrinkling my notes and taping
them into my notebook and was up
ANOTHER half hour researching stuff
on my dad's computer.

SEARCH [can people lay eggs]

THE TIME I MADE THE BIGGEST MISTAKE OF MY LIFE

OK this is just part two of that last chapter but I got so mad writing it I kind of had to take a break. But I've gotta take some deep breaths because this chapter is gonna be even HARDER to write.

The next day during the math test I tried to use my notes to help but they were all out of order.

Plus it was hard to concentrate because Greg kept trying to ask me questions.

Some of the OTHER kids were getting stressed out about the test too because Timothy Lautner got dizzy and Ms. Beck had to take him to the nurse's office.

Well as soon as Ms. Beck left the room Greg scooted his chair real close to mine and looked over my shoulder.

I whispered to Greg to go away because he was trying to CHEAT. But Greg said it's not cheating since we were study partners and we both had the exact same information in our brains.

I guess he had a point but I still didn't feel GOOD about it.

Then Greg said he already FINISHED
his test and was only trying to make sure
I got the right answers. And that made
me feel kind of nervous because I wasn't
positive about a few of them.

So I let Greg check over my test, and
believe me if I could do everything over
again I wouldn't have LET him.

After a minute I started thinking maybe
Greg wasn't just looking over my test
to check my answers but that he was
COPYING me.

And it was too late to STOP him so I
tried to pretend it wasn't happening.

Greg pushed his chair back to its normal
spot right before Ms. Beck came back.
And when the bell rang for the end of
class she went around and collected all of
our papers.

The next day Ms. Beck gave us our tests back and I got an 89. I was kind of disappointed in myself because I usually do a lot better. But Greg got an 89 too which was a really good grade for HIM.

But if you think this chapter has a happy ending, well guess what? It DOESN'T.

When class ended everyone got up to leave but Ms. Beck told me and Greg to stay in our seats.

After everyone left Ms. Beck told us she wanted to talk to us about our tests. She said she noticed we got the same grade and we got the same answers right.

But Greg said that made SENSE because we were study partners and we knew all the same stuff.

I felt pretty glad Greg was my friend because he's real good at explaining stuff like that to grown-ups.

I thought Ms. Beck was gonna let us leave but she DIDN'T. She said it seemed a little suspicious that our tests were IDENTICAL and she put them side by side to show us what she meant.

Well that's when I found out Greg copied EVERYTHING on my test, even my NAME.

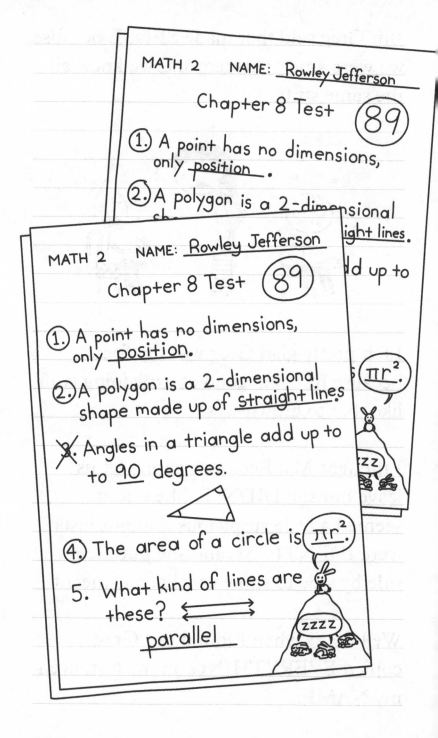

MATH 2   NAME: Rowley Jefferson

Chapter 8 Test   89

1. A point has no dimensions,
   only position.

2. A polygon is a 2-dimensional
   shape made up of straight lines.

3. Angles in a triangle add up to
   to 90 degrees.

4. The area of a circle is πr².

5. What kind of lines are
   these?
   parallel

zzzz

MATH 2   NAME: Rowley Jefferson

Chapter 8 Test   89

1. A point has no dimensions,
   only position.

2. A polygon is a 2-dimensional
   sh... ight lines.

ld up to

πr².

zzz

Ms. Beck said it was obvious that Greg copied my paper so he was gonna have to serve three days of detention PLUS he had to take the test over.

I thought Ms. Beck was gonna give me detention too but she DIDN'T. But what she said was WORSE than detention.

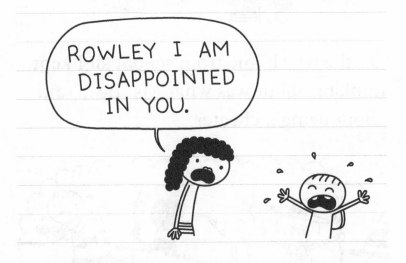

ROWLEY I AM DISAPPOINTED IN YOU.

Ms. Beck said she wanted us to learn a lesson from this and we both swore it would never happen again. Ms. Beck said well that's good because once people know you're a CHEATER it follows you wherever you go.

Then Ms. Beck said we were free to go. Greg got up and left but I gave Ms. Beck a hug to show her I was sorry. But I think maybe I hugged her for too long.

On the way home from school all I kept thinking about was what Ms. Beck said about being a cheater.

Well I learned MY lesson but I'm not so sure about Greg.

The next day Ms. Beck made Greg sit in the back of the class and retake the test. But Greg was asking me questions pretty much the whole time and I had to pretend I couldn't hear him.

And if you're like "Rowley why are you still friends with Greg?" well my answer is that Greg's still a good FRIEND, he's just a bad study partner.

Plus he's the only person I know who can lay an egg.

THE TIME GREG TOTALLY HAD MY BACK

OK Greg if you're still reading this then sorry if I made you look bad in the last two chapters. But don't worry because in this one you're gonna come out looking pretty good.

So last year our science teacher was Mrs. Modi, but when she had a baby the school got this guy named Mr. Hardy to fill in for her.

I think Mr. Hardy used to teach at the school a long time ago and now they bring him back whenever they need a long-term sub.

Mr. Hardy

I thought Mr. Hardy was just going to do things the same way as Mrs. Modi but I was WRONG. All Mr. Hardy did every day was write our assignment on the board and then read at his desk for the rest of class.

Assignment:
Do problems 1-11
on page 92.

After like the third day, kids started goofing off during class. And Mr. Hardy didn't even CARE.

One time a couple of kids tried to kill a bug by dropping their textbooks on it. Luckily the bug got away but even with all the noise Mr. Hardy never looked UP.

THUMP WHOMP

Well maybe Mr. Hardy wasn't bothered but I couldn't concentrate on my assignments with all that craziness going on every day.

Greg told me I was wasting my time doing the daily assignments because Mr. Hardy was never gonna even LOOK at them. Greg said I should just live it up with everyone ELSE until Mrs. Modi returned and things went back to normal.

Well guess what? Mrs. Modi DIDN'T come back. She decided she wanted to be a full-time mom and that meant Mr. Hardy was our teacher for the rest of the YEAR.

Now that Mr. Hardy was our official science teacher I thought things would get better. But they got WORSE.

Then on the last day of school Mr. Hardy announced he was gonna give everyone their GRADES. Well that freaked out most of the kids in my class because just about everyone in there deserved an "F."

Mr. Hardy started going down the aisles and whispering each kid's grade in their ear. But Mr. Hardy doesn't have a whispering voice so everybody else could hear what he was saying.

The first kid to get his grade was Dennis Diterlizzi and he got a "C." But Mr. Hardy talks real slow so it sounded more like this:

The next kid got a "C" too and so did every kid after that. Even Greg got a "C" and he didn't turn in a single assignment. And he was real happy about it because he didn't wanna go to summer school.

So then it was MY turn and I was kind of crossing my fingers hoping I'd get a GOOD grade. But I got the same grade as everyone ELSE.

So I guess Greg was right that Mr. Hardy never looked at those assignments.

Mr. Hardy moved on to the next kid but all of a sudden Greg stood up and argued with Mr. Hardy. Greg told him I was the only kid who did any work and that he's a terrible teacher and that someone should report him to the PRINCIPAL.

I was pretty shocked because Greg never stood up for me like that before. For a second I thought Mr. Hardy was gonna send GREG to the principal.

But after a minute Mr. Hardy whispered the NEW grade in my ear.

On the walk home I told Greg he was
a great pal for doing that for me. And
I said now we were even for that time I
saved him from Tevin Larkin's birthday
party.

But Greg said what he did for me was
WAY better than getting him out of
Tevin's party. He said by getting me
that "B" he probably just saved me from
getting some crummy job later on in life.

So I said OK how much more do I have to do until we're EVEN? And then he drew a chart to show me.

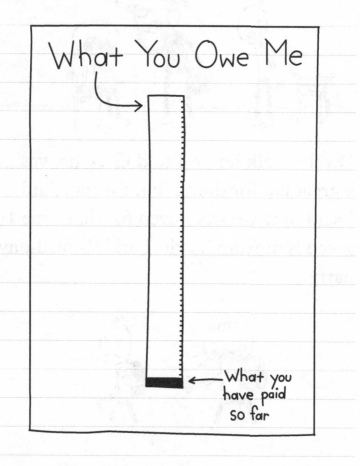

I guess that means I've got a long way to go. But that's OK because me and Greg are gonna be friends for a long time and I'll get a lot of chances to pay him back.

126

THE TIME I REALIZED MAYBE GREG DOESN'T ALWAYS TELL THE TRUTH

So after that time me and Greg were study partners I asked him how the heck he laid that egg and he told me he can lay any kind of egg he WANTS.

And I said OK then lay an OSTRICH egg, and he said for that he'd need to eat a lot of potato chips and then he took some of mine.

But a few days later when I stopped by Greg's house to pick him up for school his mom gave him an egg for his lunch. And then I remembered Greg ALWAYS has a hard-boiled egg for lunch and so he must've had one in his coat pocket the night we studied together.

Well that made me start to wonder if some OTHER stuff I know about Greg isn't true. We've been friends a long time and he's told me a BUNCH of things that seemed a little shaky so now I'm kind of thinking not everything he's told me is a hundred percent accurate.

Here are a few things I'm starting to wonder about.

1. Greg says he is dating a supermodel but they have to keep it a secret since her career would get ruined if people found out she was dating a middle school kid.

Greg said whenever she goes on TV she sends him secret messages by blinking.

2. Greg says that one time he threw a Frisbee and the wind took it so far that it went all the way around the world and hit him in the back of the head so that's why he won't play sports anymore.

3. Greg says that the "star" on the dial pad of a phone is really a SNOWFLAKE and it's a direct line to the North Pole. So whenever I do something Greg doesn't like he tells me he's gonna report me to Santa.

4. Greg says that when he was a baby his mom brought him to a modeling agency and they took some pictures for diaper cream ads.

Greg said the ads never ran in the United States but that if he went to China he'd get totally MOBBED.

5. Greg says that he came up with the "DE-FENSE" chant at basketball games and every time a crowd says it he gets one hundred dollars sent to his bank account.

6. Greg says he's 500 years old but he doesn't age and he has to move every few years so no one will figure it out. He says he knew Abraham Lincoln in middle school and he was kind of a jerk.

7. Greg says there's a form you can fill out at town hall to legally adopt any kid you want, and that he adopted me so now I have to do whatever he tells me.

8. Greg says that he can turn into any form of water whenever he wants, but when I asked him to turn into a glass of water he said the LAST time he did that Rodrick drank him and it took two days to get back to human form.

9. Greg says he only uses five percent of his brain, and if he WANTED to he could levitate a building with his mind. I said maybe I could levitate a building too but he said probably not because I'm already using one hundred percent of my brain.

10. Speaking of BRAINS, Greg says he's got ESP and he always knows what I'm gonna do before I do it.

That one might actually be true because I've seen him do it a bunch of times.

Anyway I'm guessing at least HALF this stuff is made up but I'm just writing it down here in case it ISN'T.

And for the record Greg's been eating a LOT of my potato chips over the last three weeks and there's still no ostrich egg.

THE TIME ME AND GREG CAME UP WITH OUR OWN SUPERHERO

OK this is probably gonna be the best chapter in this book because it's the only one that's got superheroes in it. And I hope I didn't spoil the surprise but even if I did, trust me it's still gonna be a pretty good chapter.

This one day it was raining so me and Greg couldn't go outside. And Greg wasn't allowed to play video games because he lost his temper playing Twisted Wizard.

Mrs. Heffley said kids our age spend too much time in front of screens anyway and it was good for us to take a break.

Then she gave us some markers and a sketchbook and told us we should use our imaginations and make up our own comics like we USED to.

Well the LAST time me and Greg made some comics together it didn't turn out so good for me. And if you don't know the whole story then I'll give you the short version.

In our first year of middle school me and Greg worked on a comic together called "Zoo-Wee Mama."

But then Greg got bored of it and said I should do it by MYSELF.

And then my comic got in the school paper and Greg was mad at me even though he's the one who TOLD me I should do it.

Then we got in a big fight in front of the whole school and some teenagers came out of NOWHERE and they caught me and Greg.

Then they made me eat a piece of _____ that was on the blacktop.

I still can't eat pizza or mozzarella sticks
or anything else with _____ in it but
Greg says I need to "get over it" because
that happened a long time ago.

So anyway when I opened that
sketchbook Mrs. Heffley gave us, there
were a bunch of Zoo-Wee Mamas in
there that we never turned in to the
school paper.

Greg said I should put them in here
because they were gonna be worth a lot
of money when he gets famous.

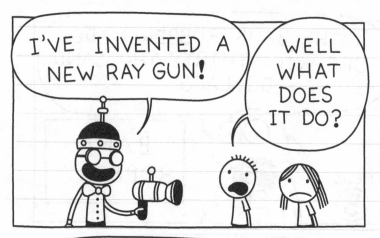

I told Greg maybe we should write some MORE Zoo-Wee Mamas but he said that joke is stale and we need to come up with something NEW.

And then Greg had an AWESOME idea. He said we should create our own SUPERHERO. Well I liked that idea a lot because it sounded FUN. But Greg said that he didn't care about having fun, he just cared about the MONEY.

Greg said that if you come up with a superhero then you can sell the movie rights and sit back and wait for the money to roll in.

Then we started talking about what we'd
do with all the money we were gonna
make from our superhero idea. I said I'd
go to the toy aisle at the store and I'd fill
up a shopping cart with as many toys as I
could fit.

But Greg said I wasn't thinking BIG
enough. He said he'd buy the whole
STORE and wear a different pair of
sneakers every day and he'd live in the
snacks aisle.

Then I said I'd buy a fancy sports car and I'd give Ms. Beck a ride to school every morning.

Greg said we were gonna be so rich we could buy the whole SCHOOL and fire all the teachers and have epic paintball fights in the hallways.

I said maybe we shouldn't fire ALL of the teachers because Ms. Beck is really nice and she's good at teaching math.

Greg said we'd be so rich we wouldn't NEED to learn math anymore but we could keep Ms. Beck around because we'd need someone to count our money for us. And I guess that made me feel a little better.

Greg said we had PLENTY of time to figure out what we were gonna do with all our money later ON but right now it was time to get serious about this superhero idea.

Greg said the FIRST thing we needed to do was figure out what kind of POWERS our superhero should have.

150

I said maybe he could fly or have superstrength but Greg said both of those ideas were dumb because they've been done a million times before.

Then I said maybe our superhero could have x-ray vision but Greg said that wasn't a good superpower because once he accidentally saw his grandpa naked and he wishes he HADN'T.

Greg said we needed to do something ORIGINAL so we started coming up with ideas that no one ever THOUGHT of before. And the ideas we came up with were OK but not great.

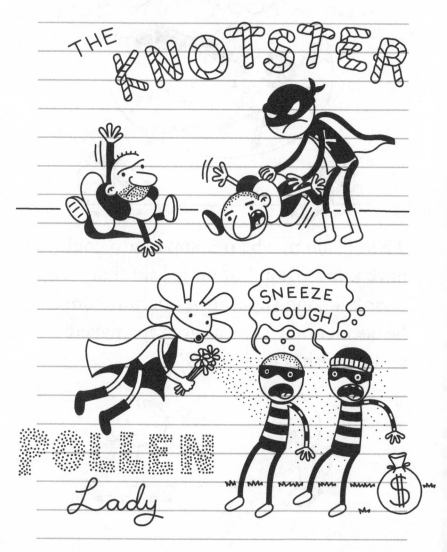

The one we liked the best was this guy called the Chuckster who could throw his own HEAD like a football.

But Greg said the Chuckster wouldn't work as an action figure because the head would be a choking hazard for little kids.

154

Then we tried to come up with some characters that WOULD be OK if a kid accidentally swallowed them but most of our ideas weren't that good.

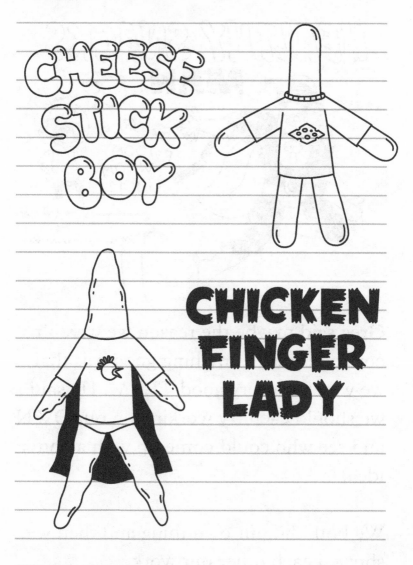

CHEESE STICK BOY

CHICKEN FINGER LADY

Greg said moms are usually the ones who buy their kids toys so we should come up with something THEY'D like. But we weren't happy with that idea either.

Greg said maybe the reason we weren't coming up with anything good was that we weren't a very good TEAM. He said we should each try working on our OWN and see who could come up with a better idea.

We both did our own thing and then we showed each other our work.

Greg's superhero was a guy from space who had a different kind of power in every fingertip which was actually a pretty awesome idea.

I told Greg his idea was cool and we should go with THAT.

Then Greg said well what's YOUR idea? But I didn't wanna tell him because I knew he'd laugh. And then he promised he WOULDN'T laugh so I showed him my character.

Greg asked what Amazing Guy's superpower was and I said it was KINDNESS. And that made Greg break his promise about not laughing.

Greg said a superhero should be EDGY and it would be cool if Amazing Guy had knives coming out of his knuckles and wore a black leather jacket and said swears when he fights the bad guys.

But I said I wanted Amazing Guy to be a role model for children, and that made Greg break his promise a second time.

POUND
POUND

I told Greg if he didn't like my character that was fine but I wasn't giving him any money if I sold the MOVIE rights. And all of a sudden Greg got real interested in Amazing Guy and said if I get rich I owe him half the money because I used his markers and paper.

I said that wasn't true and Greg said he'd call his lawyer to find out. Then Greg dialed a number on the phone and I listened in on his half of the conversation.

MM HMM. YEP, THEY'RE MY MARKERS. FIFTY PERCENT? OK THAT'S WHAT I THOUGHT.

Then Greg hung up the phone. I told him to call his lawyer BACK because I wanted to ask him a few questions.

But Greg said I couldn't AFFORD his lawyer and I had to get my own.

Greg said since we were gonna split things 50-50 then we were equal partners and we needed to work TOGETHER. I said fine but I still don't want Amazing Guy to say swears and Greg said OK we'll talk about that later.

Greg said the FIRST thing we needed to do was give Amazing Guy an "origin story" to show how he got his powers. Then he told me how OTHER superheroes got their powers.

I said Amazing Guy just had good parents who raised him to be a nice person and that's why he decided when he grew up he'd fight for people who needed his help.

But Greg said that's a TERRIBLE origin story. He said something EXCITING needed to happen, like Amazing Guy gets hit by a meteor or gets bitten by a radioactive bug or something like that.

And I said OK fine then Amazing Guy gets hit by a double rainbow and THAT'S how he gets his powers.

Greg said that didn't make SENSE but he didn't feel like getting into a dumb argument about rainbows so we'd come back to the origin story later on too.

Greg said every good superhero has a secret identity so we needed to come up with one for Amazing Guy.

I said he could be a nurse at an urgent care clinic and when he gets off work at 6:00 p.m. he becomes Amazing Guy and then helps people until his bedtime.

And no one knows his secret identity, not even Nurse Beck who works with him at the urgent care place.

Greg said I got that name from Ms. Beck our math teacher but I said nope it's just a coincidence.

Greg said we were wasting too much time talking about stupid stuff and we needed to design Amazing Guy's SUIT.

I said I liked the suit I came up with just FINE but Greg said it was stupid because everyone could tell who he was if they saw him walking around in regular life.

Greg said Amazing Guy needed a mask, so he drew one that looked pretty awesome. And he added a cape too.

Then Greg said if Amazing Guy doesn't have any real powers then maybe his SUIT could have powers. But I said Amazing Guy has the power of KINDNESS and his gloves are padded so he doesn't hurt the bad guys too much.

I said I wanted to do all the drawings and Greg said that's fine but he'd do the WRITING. So I drew this awesome scene where Amazing Guy has to leave work early to go fight some bad guys and I left space for Greg to fill in the words.

I told Greg he totally messed up my comic and that from now on I'd do the drawing AND the writing. Then Greg said he was gonna call his lawyer again and I said go right AHEAD. And even when he said he was gonna call SANTA I wouldn't budge.

Greg said he didn't want to write for my stupid comic anyway because my superhero was terrible and he said he was just gonna write Intergalactic Man comics and I said fine because my character was BETTER.

Then Greg said if Intergalactic Man got in a fight with Amazing Guy he'd wipe him out in like five seconds. And I said oh yeah let's see about THAT. So then we drew this battle and he drew HIS superhero and I drew MINE.

I guess I got a little carried away with that last drawing because after I drew it Greg said it was probably time for me to go home.

Maybe next time I won't have Amazing Guy use his FULL powers on his enemies. Because I wouldn't want his parents or Nurse Beck to be disappointed in him.

THE TIME ME AND GREG HAD A TWO-NIGHT SLEEPOVER

OK you already know this from the title of the chapter, but this one time me and Greg had a TWO-NIGHT SLEEPOVER. And I bet you think we had a total blast and you want to read about all the wacky stuff we did, but guess what? It was not that fun at ALL.

The reason this sleepover happened was because my Nana got sick and me and my parents were gonna go visit her but then Mrs. Heffley said:

WHY DON'T YOU TWO GO AND WE'LL WATCH ROWLEY FOR THE WEEKEND?

When my mom said OK to that idea,
me and Greg were HYPED because we
never had a two-night sleepover before.
But I guess we should've waited until
later to celebrate because of the whole
Nana thing.

On Friday my mom packed my bag for
the weekend and she put in an extra pair
of underwear "just in case."

Plus she packed a picture of her and my
dad so I could look at it if I missed them
too much while they were gone.

Like I said before, the sleepover wasn't a lot of fun but it started off pretty good. We played video games in Greg's basement and ate snacks. Then we prank-called Scotty Douglas and he blew the whistle he keeps right by his phone for when we do that.

EXCUSE ME SIR YOUR REFRIGERATOR IS RUNNING SO MAYBE YOU SHOULD GO CATCH IT.

TWEET

But then Mrs. Douglas called Mrs. Heffley to tell on us for prank-calling Scotty. Then Mrs. Heffley told us we were "bullying" and that made me feel ashamed.

At 9:00 Mrs. Heffley said it was time for bed and she went back upstairs.

I was pretty tired but Greg said he had an idea. There is this kid on our street named Joseph O'Rourke who has a trampoline but he never lets anyone use it. Greg said we should sneak out and jump on the trampoline while Joe was asleep.

Well I wasn't so crazy about this sneaking-out idea but Greg said if I was going to be a baby I should go up to Manny's room and sleep in THERE.

I said I wasn't a baby and he said "Yuh-huh" and I said "Nuh-uh." Then he said "Yuh-huh times INFINITY" but I was ready for that and I said "Nuh-uh times infinity SQUARED." And I thought I had Greg beat with that one, but he got me anyway when he said "Yuh-huh times infinity squared plus ONE."

So we snuck out the back door and I followed Greg up to Joe's. It was really cold outside and all I had on were my jammies, but I didn't wanna complain because then Greg might call me a baby again.

Sure enough all the lights at the O'Rourkes' house were off so this was our big chance to use Joe's trampoline. Greg said we couldn't make any noise and then he climbed up and did a bunch of jumps but he was real quiet.

Then it was MY turn. This was my first time on a trampoline and it was REALLY fun, and I guess that's why I forgot we were being sneaky.

The lights came on inside the O'Rourkes' house and their dog started barking and Greg took off without me. I wanted to run TOO but it's not so easy to stop bouncing when you're on a trampoline.

Once I finally stopped I ran to the Heffleys' house and went around back to the basement door.

But I guess Greg wanted to teach me a
lesson for making too much noise at the
O'Rourkes' because he wouldn't let me in.

I tried to show Greg that I was freezing
but I don't think he really got what I was
trying to tell him.

I thought he was gonna make me stay
out there all NIGHT so I ran around
the house to see if the front door was
unlocked.

But it WASN'T and I kind of freaked out
a little.

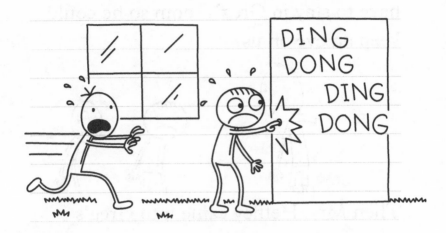

The good news is that someone came to
the door pretty quick but the bad news is
that it was Mr. Heffley.

Mr. Heffley told us to get our stuff from the basement because we were gonna have to stay in Greg's room so he could keep an eye on us.

Then Mrs. Heffley came into Greg's room and said she was disappointed in us for sneaking out and that made me feel ashamed all over again. But I think Greg gets in trouble a LOT because he didn't seem that ashamed.

As soon as Mrs. Heffley went to bed, Greg said I was dumb for making all that noise at the O'Rourkes' and EXTRA dumb for ringing the doorbell. I said I was sorry for saying "wheeee" on the trampoline but the doorbell thing was all his fault.

Then Greg whapped me with his pillow and I whapped him BACK but I guess we made too much noise and that's why I had to see Mr. Heffley in his underwear for the second time in one night.

Mr. Heffley told Greg he had to sleep in Manny's room and all I could think was, who's the baby NOW?

The next day Mrs. Heffley woke me up and said breakfast was ready downstairs.

Greg was in the bathroom brushing his teeth and he said he hoped I brought my own toothpaste because if I wanted to use his I was gonna have to pay for it since it was his house.

I told him I DID have my own toothpaste and then he said I was gonna have to pay for the water I used to brush my teeth.

I said I wasn't gonna pay for the water because I was the guest and guests are supposed to get treated SPECIAL.

So he said if I wasn't gonna pay what I owed I couldn't eat breakfast or any other meals either.

I was like yeah RIGHT and then he said I was using his electricity and he shut the light off on me.

When I got downstairs I told Mrs. Heffley about all the stuff Greg said upstairs and she said I was RIGHT about guests being special.

Then she let me pick which pancakes I
wanted before Greg got to pick.

After breakfast Mrs. Heffley said we had
too much screen time the day before and
that we had to figure out something to do
until lunch.

Greg was in a grumpy mood so I decided
to cheer him up with a knock-knock joke.
But he wouldn't do the "who's there"
part no matter how many times I tried.

I told Greg I was gonna go upstairs and tell his mom he wasn't saying "who's there." And that finally made him do it.

I said what do elephants do at night? But Greg said you're not supposed to ask a question in that part of a knock-knock joke and I said yes you are.

Then he told me I was dumb and I said I was gonna tell on him for THAT. And Greg said go right ahead and so I DID.

So Mrs. Heffley came down and told
Greg he wasn't allowed to call me dumb
or stupid or any other bad names either.

But then when she left, Greg said he had
a new nickname for me. At first I thought
it sounded cool but then I figured out
what he MEANT.

HEY
STOOP.

I told Greg I was gonna tell on him
AGAIN but then Greg said that it was
Opposite Day and everything meant the
opposite of what it was supposed to.

Well I knew what he MEANT so I went
and told Mrs. Heffley. But at first she
didn't get mad because she didn't know
it was Opposite Day.

I explained it to Mrs. Heffley and she made Greg apologize. But I think he might've been being opposite.

Mrs. Heffley told us that sometimes friends get on each other's nerves but we needed to figure things out since we had a whole day to go on our sleepover.

She said maybe we should spend some time apart and I thought that sounded like a GREAT idea. So I hung out with Manny in his room for a while.

Even though I was having fun with Manny, I missed my mom and dad and I looked at their picture whenever I got the chance.

WHIMPER

The next time I saw Greg was when we had lunch. Mrs. Heffley made peanut butter and jelly sandwiches and she even remembered to cut the crusts off mine.

After we finished our sandwiches she gave us chocolate chip cookies for dessert. She gave Greg one but she gave me TWO because she said I was the guest and guests are SPECIAL.

I ate one of my cookies but I made a shield around the other cookie with my arms so Greg couldn't get it. Sometimes if I have something Greg wants he will lick it so I won't want it anymore.

That's what he did last Halloween when
I got more candy than he did.

But Greg said he was full and didn't even
WANT my cookie. He said that while I
was playing with Manny he was reading
a book about magic and he wanted to
show me a trick. I really like magic so I
said OK.

First Greg told me to put my fingers on
the edge of the table so they were close
together like this:

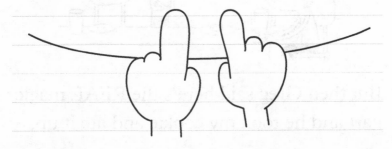

Then Greg took my glass of milk and put it on top of my fingers.

I asked him when the magic part was gonna happen and he said it was ALREADY happening because I couldn't move. Well he was right because if I did, the glass of milk would tip over and spill. And Mr. Heffley gets mad when I spill stuff in his house.

But then Greg said here's the REAL magic part and he took my cookie and ate it up.

GOBBLE
GOBBLE

After that, Greg went upstairs but I was stuck at the kitchen table. And I was still there a half hour later when Mrs. Heffley came back to the kitchen.

I told her what Greg did and boy was she mad but it wasn't because of the magic trick. She was mad that Greg took something that belonged to me without asking.

We went up to Greg's room and then
Mrs. Heffley told me I could pick out
one of Greg's things to take home with
me so we'd be even.

Well Greg had a BUNCH of cool toys
that he never let me play with so it was
really hard to pick. But every time I got
close to one of his favorites he kind of let
me know I shouldn't pick that one.

I picked an action figure that was a
knight with a missing arm and Greg
seemed OK with that.

But as soon as Mrs. Heffley left the room
Greg said I could play with my lame
action figure because he was gonna play
with all his cool stuff by himself.

It kind of bugged me and I wanted to bug Greg BACK. So I pretended I was having a total blast with my toy.

Well it WORKED and Greg said I had to hand over his toy. I said no way and he said he was just gonna wait for me to fall asleep and he'd take it back HIMSELF.

I told him I was gonna put the action figure down my underwear so he couldn't get it and he didn't like that idea.

Then Greg said he'd TRADE me for
the action figure and I asked him what
he'd give me for it. Greg said he'd give
me ninety-nine cents for the knight and I
said OK to that.

But then Greg took a dirty sock out of
his hamper and tried to get me to smell
it.

And I was like what was that for? And
Greg said that was my first "scent."

I said I wanted ninety-nine CENTS not ninety-nine SCENTS. But Greg said a deal's a deal and then he tried to get me to smell another sock as my second scent.

When I told Greg I was gonna go tell on him again, he said he'd trade me his Lego dragon for my knight and I said YES because that dragon is way better than a knight with no arm.

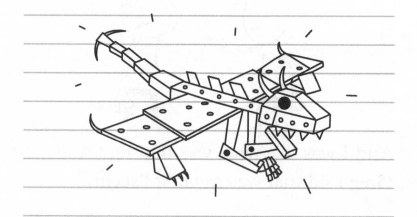

But then when I gave Greg my knight he wouldn't give me the dragon because he said I should've remembered it was still Opposite Day.

Well that was the last straw for me and I tried to grab the dragon from Greg. But it kind of slipped out of my hands and hit the floor and broke apart.

CLATTER CLATTER

I guess we were making a lot of noise because the next thing we knew Greg's mom was back in the room. She said she was gonna have to separate us for the rest of the night which was fine with ME.

Mrs. Heffley said that we each had one half of the bedroom and that we had to stay on our own side. So she asked me which side I wanted and I picked the side with the BED which made Greg mad.

When Mrs. Heffley went back to her room, Greg said he was turning on an invisible force field between our two sides.

Then he said if someone crossed over they'd get zapped.

Greg said he was fine with me having the bed because he could sleep on an air mattress and plus all the fun stuff was on HIS side of the room. And when I reached over to Greg's side for my action figure, sure enough I got zapped.

I opened the drawer in the table next to Greg's bed to see if he had any comics I could read. Well there weren't any comics but one of Greg's old handheld video games was in there.

So I played it and Greg couldn't do anything because of the force field.

But Greg said I could play video games by myself like a nerd because he was having a wild party on HIS side of the room and I wasn't invited. And I got kind of jealous because his party looked pretty fun.

I said well I'm having a party on MY side and it was even more wild than HIS party and I had really good music. Greg said I couldn't even come up with an original idea but I still think he was jealous of my party.

Then Greg said the plug to my party speakers was on HIS side of the room so he pulled it out to shut off my music.

Greg got back to his party and I tried to tell him to plug my speakers back in but Greg couldn't hear me because the music at his party was too loud.

But this time MR. Heffley came into
the room and Greg didn't notice him
standing in the doorway.

Mr. Heffley said he didn't want one more
peep out of us and then he left the room.
We were both quiet for a long time but
then Greg tried to get me to laugh and I
almost did.

I was kind of glad we had to be quiet
because I was getting pretty sleepy
anyway and I wanted to go to bed.

I told Greg I needed to brush my teeth
and he said too bad because the force
field was still on and I was trapped in my
half of the room for the whole night.

So I asked if he could just turn off the
force field for a little while so I could
brush my teeth but he said once the force
field is turned on it stays on until the
morning.

And then Greg went to the bathroom to
brush HIS teeth and came back to the
room after he was done.

That's when I remembered I need to use the bathroom before I go to bed every night so I don't have any accidents.

But Greg said I was just gonna have to hold it until the morning. I said I couldn't MAKE it all the way to morning and Greg said that wasn't his problem.

I said if Greg didn't shut off the force field I was gonna have to pee in the Chewbacca mug on the table next to Greg's bed. Then he told me he had a special invisible knife that could cut through the force field.

Greg showed me how the knife worked by cutting a square in the force field right next to the table where the mug was.

Then he reached through the hole and grabbed the mug.

I asked Greg to cut a Rowley-sized hole in the force field so I could get through it to use the bathroom.

But Greg said the knife ran on
invisible batteries and they got used up
when he made HIS hole so I was out
of luck.

Then Greg started talking about all
sorts of things that made me feel like I
really needed to use the bathroom.

Finally Greg got tired and he fell
asleep. I thought about trying to sneak
past him but I was worried he was just
faking it and I was gonna get zapped.

After a while I fell asleep too. But I woke up around six in the morning feeling like I was gonna BURST.

I didn't care about the force field anymore but I was worried that if I used the bathroom I might wake up Mr. Heffley. But I should've just used the bathroom anyway because Mr. Heffley was already up for the day.

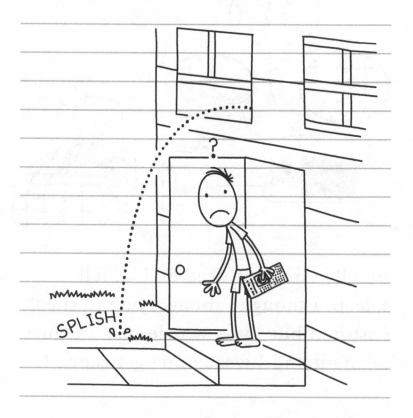

Luckily Mr. Heffley didn't look up in time to see me in the window and when he got to Greg's room I was already back in bed.

I fell back asleep after a while and got up when Mrs. Heffley said it was time for breakfast.

After we ate, I went to get my knight action figure from Greg's room but I couldn't find the toy ANYWHERE.

Greg said he didn't know what happened to it, but Mrs. Heffley said he had to help me look for it.

So the two of us searched Greg's room but to be honest he wasn't all that helpful.

I guess Mrs. Heffley thought Greg was hiding the action figure from me because she said if he didn't hand it over in two minutes then he was gonna be in big trouble.

Greg said he needed to use the bathroom but he'd keep looking for my action figure after he was done. But I noticed he had something in his hand when he went in there.

Greg locked the bathroom door and Mrs. Heffley told him to come out right this instant. But then the toilet flushed and when Greg opened the door there wasn't anything in his hand anymore.

Mrs. Heffley made Greg give me THREE toys and this time I picked out ones that WEREN'T broken.

My mom and dad came and got me just before lunch and boy was I glad to see them. And P.S. if you wanted to know the answer to that knock-knock joke, it's "Elephants watch elevision."

THE ADVENTURES OF
GREG AND ROWLEY

I'm pretty much up to date on Greg's life
so today I showed Greg what I wrote so
far. I thought he would like it but he was
MAD.

Greg said this book was supposed to be
about HIM and not about ME. I told
him it was hard to write about just HIM
because most of the time we do stuff
TOGETHER.

He said I need to go back through the
book and take out all the stuff with me
in it. I told him that would be dumb
because then the book would only be like
one page long.

I said maybe we should change the title to "THE ADVENTURES OF GREG AND ROWLEY" and it could be OUR biography.

Then I said since there's a lot of scary stuff in this book we could make it into a spooky series where these two pals solve mysteries. We could make a lot of money and we'd BOTH be rich and famous.

Greg said that was the stupidest idea he ever heard.

He said this book is about HIS life and if he wants to he can change the name of Greg's best friend to "Rupert" and then he wouldn't owe me ANYTHING. Plus he said he'd make Rupert really dumb and drooling all the time.

Then Greg told me the book smelled
funny anyway and when I brought it up
to my nose to sniff it he closed the book
on my face.

So I said hey what was THAT for? and
Greg said that's what I got for dropping
him in the puddle.

Then he said he got me back when I
least expected it and I guess he was right
about THAT.

But I was pretty mad and I whapped him
with his own biography.

WHAP

Well I guess Greg wasn't expecting
THAT because he lost his balance and
fell in a big puddle.

Anyway I am up in my room now and I am hoping Greg's mom calls him home for bedtime soon because he already skipped dinner.

I'm glad all that stuff happened today because it gave me a whole new chapter in our biography. I'm sure we'll be pals again tomorrow and we'll have a bunch of new adventures that I can put in here.

And I'll bet if we go with my idea about the scary stuff it'll sell a million copies.

But if Greg changes my name to Rupert I just want to say for the record that he wet his pants at that first sleepover too.

OK Now Back to This Being About Me

Well if Greg's not happy with his biography then I can go back to using this journal to write about MYSELF.

So now I'm officially the main character of this book again. And from now on this thing is just gonna be about me and my mom and my dad and I might mention Ms. Beck one more time if there's enough room.

Speaking of my mom and dad, after my last fight with Greg they came to my room to talk about it.

ROWLEY MAYBE IT'S TIME TO FIND SOME NEW FRIENDS.

But I don't really think I can add any new friends because Greg takes up so much of my time.

I know me and Greg don't always get along but like Mrs. Heffley said, sometimes friends get on each other's nerves.

Well me and Greg get on each other's nerves a LOT so I guess that just proves that we're

I TOLD YOU IT WAS GONNA BE BAD!

ABOUT THE AUTHOR

Jeff Kinney is a #1 *New York Times* best-selling author of the Diary of a Wimpy Kid Series and six-time Nickelodeon Kids' Choice Award winner for Favorite Book. Jeff has been named one of *Time* magazine's 100 Most Influential People in the World. He is also the creator of Poptropica, which was named one of *Time's* 50 Best Websites. He spent his childhood in the Washington, D.C., area and moved to New England in 1995. Jeff lives with his wife and two sons in Plainville, Massachusetts, where they own An Unlikely Story Bookstore & Cafe.